STOP THE BALLOON!

STOP THE BALLOON!

AND OTHER ADVENTURE STORIES

Compiled by the Editors of Highlights for Children

BOYDS MILLS PRESS

Published by Boyds Mills Press, Inc.
A Highlights Company
815 Church Street
Honesdale, Pennsylvania 18431
Printed in the United States of America

Publisher Cataloging-in-Publication Data
Main entry under title.
Stop the balloon! : and other adventure stories /
compiled by the editors of *Highlights for Children.*
[96]p. : cm.
Stories originally published in *Highlights for Children.*
Summary: A collection of adventure stories.
ISBN 1-56397-194-1
1. Adventure stories—Juvenile fiction. [1. Adventure stories.]
I. Highlights for Children. II. Title.
[F] 1993
Library of Congress Catalog Card Number: 92-73625

First edition, 1993
Book designed by Tim Gillner
The text of this book is set in 12-point Garamond.
Distributed by St. Martin's Press

10 9 8 7 6 5 4 3

CONTENTS

Stop the Balloon!

By Kathleen Stevens

Tally gave a last look up the lane. She fancied she could still see her brother Charlie riding away toward the hollow where he was to meet the other cavalrymen.

"I hope to be back soon, Tally," he had said. "Once we get news of the Yankees' weak spot to General Lee, he'll soon have them chased all the way back to Washington."

Tally was about to return to the house. But what was that? Men on horseback. The creak of wagon wheels, too.

Tally dashed for the house. "Mother, strangers

are coming in the lane!"

Tally's mother looked out the door. "Yankees, maybe. Hunting for food. Charlie left just in time with the supplies and equipment. They'll find nothing worth taking left here." Her mother's glance fell on the long wooden table where she and Tally had stitched the trousers and jackets Charlie had just carried off. "Quick, Tally—the needle and shears." She hid the precious needle in a crack and handed Tally the shears. Darting upstairs to the loft, Tally placed them in their hiding place under a loose board.

By the time Tally returned, more than a dozen men had ridden into the yard. Behind them rattled a wagon that looked like a boxcar on wheels. At the top of the strange vehicle she could see some kind of pipe.

"That's the balloon wagon!" Tally gasped.

The Yankees' new weapon was a balloon so big it could carry a man into the air to spy on the Confederate army. Confederate cannons had tried to destroy the balloon but so far hadn't succeeded.

A man with a telescope slung over his shoulder walked toward the house. "Good evening, ladies. I am Professor Thaddeus Lowe, Chief of Aeronautics of the Union Army."

Tally listened as Lowe explained that the soldiers planned to stay the night and use the Paynes' yard as a launch site in the morning.

Already the soldiers had begun to set up camp. Tally watched them unload a crumpled mass of silk, netted with ropes, and link it to the wagon. As gas seeped in, the orange mass slowly swelled. The soldiers fastened long cords around stout pegs in the ground to hold the balloon in place.

"At dawn we'll finish filling the balloon," Professor Lowe explained. "Then I'll ascend for an early morning view of your lovely countryside."

"And our good men in gray," Tally's mother said sharply.

Tally stifled a gasp. What if Professor Lowe saw her brother and the other cavalrymen? Could the Yankees head them off before they got back to Richmond with news of the Yankees' weak spot?

"Now," said Professor Lowe with a bow, "I regret that I must order you ladies to spend the night upstairs."

In the loft, with the trapdoor locked behind them, Tally's mother turned to her. "Tally," she whispered, "we must delay the balloon flight until Charlie and the other men have had time to get back to Richmond."

They hurried to the front window. Tally stared at the half-filled balloon drifting in the evening breeze. "Maybe I could cut the balloon loose."

Her mother shook her head. "It isn't full enough to blow away. Besides, they'd surely catch you if you tried to cut all the cords. But if you cut just one—look, Tally!"

Staring at the trees across the yard, Tally saw what her mother meant. Excitedly they made plans.

For a long time boots creaked across the floor below. At last all was silent. Her mother helped Tally out the rear window. "Be careful," she whispered.

Tally's bare feet edged along the shed roof, the shears dangling from her waist by a piece of ribbon. She dropped to the ground and ran, crouching, toward the bushes at the edge of the yard. Keeping behind the bushes, Tally circled the house.

By the campfire one soldier stood guard while the others slept. Ahead, the half-filled balloon swayed in the night air. Tally moved forward until she saw a cord glimmering in the moonlight. She eased the blades of the shears over the heavy cord and squeezed as hard as she could. Snap! The cord yanked across the ground as the breeze tugged the balloon.

The surprised sentry turned toward the sound. The half-filled balloon was shifting toward the trees. "Grab it!" he yelled, racing frantically after the trailing cord.

Heart thumping, Tally scurried through the shadows toward the back of the house. Behind her she heard excited yells—"It's loose!" "Watch out for the branches."

Her mother waited on the roof, ready to grab Tally's hand. Together they tumbled through the window, and her mother pulled a long nightgown over Tally's head, covering her clothes. Downstairs, footsteps clattered as Professor Lowe and his men rushed out to see what had happened.

From the front window Tally and her mother watched men scurry back and forth shouting orders. Tally choked down a giggle as she saw the balloon thoroughly tangled in the trees. "It will take a long time to get it loose," her mother whispered. "They can't pull too hard—they might tear the balloon."

Suddenly footsteps thudded on the stairs. Tally and her mother dived for bed, pulling the covers up to their chins.

Professor Lowe rose through the trapdoor, lifting a lantern overhead.

"Trouble?" Tally's mother asked.

"An accident," the professor said angrily. "The balloon broke loose. Don't worry. We'll get it fixed."

But not for a while, Tally thought with satisfaction as the flickering light vanished through the opening. Not in time to see the Southern cavalrymen ride at dawn for Richmond. A woman and a ten-year-old girl had seen to that!

The High Bridge

By Maureen Dunne

Aila stared up at the snowy peaks of the Himalayas. Today Nepal's high ranges were clear. The mountains—the highest in the world—rose up and up.

Aila sighed and looked back to the village. Everybody was busy and excited. Three of their Sherpa men were leaving to guide climbers to Everest—the highest peak of all. Everybody was happy. Everybody but Aila. And he should be the happiest because his father was the lead guide.

Well, he was. But Aila was ashamed, too. His father was brave. He climbed high where the air was thin and there were crevasses and cliffs. And he, Aila, was frightened of height.

Aila was sure his father wished he weren't such a baby about heights. Aila wished it himself, but wishing didn't help. Whenever he got near a cliff or had to cross one of Nepal's swinging bridges, his head seemed to go around in circles.

His father hurried toward Aila and then grinned and waved his hand toward the soaring mountains.

"Tomorrow," he said, "I will be there." He pointed at the bottom of the mountains. "And the next day, perhaps there." He raised his finger a fraction of an inch. "Then in a very long time—two months—three, maybe—I will be there." He pointed toward the sky.

Aila grinned back.

"And then maybe the next time," his father whispered, "you will be with the rest of us up there."

"But anyway," his father continued when Aila stared at his feet, "for this time you can come as far as the bridge over the river. Then you'll hurry back and look after little Ang for your mother. Don't let him wander away and get lost. He likes to walk too much." He hugged Aila's two-year-old brother and then hoisted up his eighty-pound pack.

"Time to go," he said. "Come, Aila."

"Yes, Father," Aila said eagerly. He walked happily beside the men on the dirt track. "And I'll do what you say. No need to worry." He glanced again at the rugged mountains. "Does it feel good, Father, to stand there so near the sky?" he asked.

"Very good." His father nodded. "Of course I don't go all the way up. But still—you'll see one time."

Aila shook his head and walked close to the thick leafy trees, as far from the cliff as he could, when they neared the river. Even these cliffs made him dizzy.

Another twist in the trail and they were at the frail bridge. The men secured their packs so that they wouldn't slip.

"Good-bye, Father," Aila said.

His father waved and then eased across the long, twisted bamboo bridge. Aila watched him, his heart in his throat. Every time his father took a step, the bridge swung and tipped high over the river.

Aila felt dizzy just watching. Soon the men were on the far side, and Aila started back to the village through the bush off the trail. This way was shorter. Besides, he didn't want to return on the trail alone.

He jogged through the trees. Now there were

the roofs of the houses with the mountains rising behind. Aila felt better, seeing his people. For a minute he had felt as if he were almost alone in the world.

He skirted a neighbor's cottage and then dashed into his home and dropped to the floor. His mother looked up from the fire and smiled.

"Well, they are gone," Aila said. "I went as far as the bridge."

He sighed as his mother looked past him to the doorway.

"Where's Ang?" she said. "You'd better bring him in."

Aila stared at her.

"Aila," his mother said more loudly, "where is Ang?"

Aila frowned. "Ang?" he said. "I don't know. I thought he was here."

His mother shook her head. "He's not. I haven't seen him since you left. I thought you had him."

She jumped up and hurried to the door. Aila ran after her.

"Have you seen little Ang?" she called to the neighbors. Nobody had. Aila watched them shake their heads and look at each other in concern.

Then they were all searching in different directions. More villagers ran to help. Anything might happen to Ang. He might get lost in the bush. He might fall off a cliff.

Aila thought of his chubby little brother as he ran toward the bridge. Nobody was looking here. And perhaps Ang had followed as they left the village. If he had, he would be at the river now. He loved to walk.

Aila felt sick. Nothing must happen to little Ang. It would be too terrible. Aila ran fast. Then suddenly he saw Ang's fat little footprints in the dirt.

Aila gulped for breath and ran even faster. He could hear the river now and see it.

At the bridge Aila stopped and glanced around. Then he saw the little hump halfway across. Ang! The bridge swayed gently, high over the angry water that crashed over huge boulders many yards below.

Aila's heart pounded. He could see that Ang was frightened. He wasn't moving. But if he did —one little inch—he would roll right off!

Aila started across. He had to go gently or the bridge would rock. He put each foot down slowly. He could see the water—so far below! He felt sick and dizzy. And he was only partway there.

Then little Ang started to move!

Aila let go of the bamboo rail and ran. The bridge swayed, and he stumbled. Then he reached little Ang and held him tight.

The bridge twisted and leaped—the river and the sky seemed all mixed up. Slowly the bridge stopped swinging. Then it was almost still.

"It's all right," he said to little Ang. "I've got you."

Ang smiled at Aila and then stared happily down through the holes in the bridge as Aila started to carry him back. The bridge jumped as Aila put his foot down too hard. He stood quietly and waited till it settled.

Then suddenly Aila realized that he was on the high bridge, that he'd been on it when it was swinging, and that he'd even run on it when Ang started to move. And he wasn't even dizzy! He could look down at the water and walk just like the men. He wasn't scared anymore.

When they were off the bridge, Aila looked up at the mountains and shouted with happiness. Then he hugged little Ang even tighter and ran back to the village. Everything was going to be all right!

Trouble on a Pack Trip

By P. C. Degenhart

The road was getting rougher and the country more wild as the Jeep bounced and jolted along.

Ron was tired and hungry. He and his father had left home at dawn. At first it was fun watching the mountains get closer and bigger. But all that Ron wanted now was food and sleep.

For more than a year his father had planned to pack into the rugged Trinity Alps of Northern California and photograph the rare weeping spruce trees. Ron had begged to go along.

"I've only a week to get in there and back," his father protested. "It's too hard a trip for a thirteen-year-old."

"Ron can do it. He's got courage," his mother said. "And I'll feel better if you don't go alone."

So here Ron was in the Jeep with his father, tired out already and hungry as a wolf.

"End of the road," his father called as he stopped the Jeep beside a stream. "You unroll the sleeping bags, and I'll build a fire and warm up the stew."

Ron's plate of stew went down fast. He was asleep minutes later.

His father shook him awake in the cold dawn. "It's a long pull to Canyon Lake where we'll camp tonight. Let's eat and get moving."

They followed a narrow ravine over boulders and fallen timber. As Ron toiled on and up, trying to match his father's swift pace, his legs and back began to ache. One step up, another, on and on. Then a roaring waterfall blocked their way.

"We'll climb around," his father said.

They struggled almost straight up through loose shale and thick brush. Ron slipped and fell back so many times that his father got ahead. As he tried to catch up, Ron fell.

"I don't care whether I move or not," he muttered.

Then he heard his father shout, "Here's the lake, Ron!"

Ron labored up the last few feet, then threw himself down beside the cool water.

"It was a hard hike today," his father said. "And tomorrow's will be even harder."

Ron awoke the next morning to the smell of frying bacon. They ate quickly. Then they circled the lake and started up an old, rocky trail. After a mile of steep climbing, the trail leveled off along a deep gorge.

"This looks treacherous," his father told him. "You wait here. I'll go ahead and look."

Ron sat down, grateful for the rest. He watched his father pick his way carefully over the loose shale. Then Ron leaped to his feet as he saw a rock break loose from the slope above and hurtle directly toward his father.

"Look out, Dad!" Ron yelled.

His father jumped back, but the rock smashed into his leg. He wavered, lost his balance, and slid off the trail and down into the gorge.

Gone was Ron's weariness. He scrambled down the side of the gorge, calling as he went. No answer. Then, near the bottom, he saw the still form of his father and ran to him.

"Dad, are you hurt badly?"

His father tried to sit up. "It's my leg. It's broken, I think." He fell back.

Ron felt a chill of fear. His father's face was white and covered with sweat. Ron got one of the sleeping bags and covered him.

"Get help." His father's voice was faint.

Get help? Where? It would take over a day to get back to the Jeep. Ron looked up at the tall mountain. A peak was not far away. He'd climb that and build a fire on top. A forest lookout would surely see the smoke.

"I'm going, Dad," he said.

"Hurry," his father mumbled.

It was a hard climb. But Ron seemed to have an inner strength that kept him going over loose shale, around big boulders, and through tangled underbrush. His breath was coming in choking gasps when he reached the top.

He rested for a moment. Then he gathered a big pile of dry wood that blazed up when he put a match to it. Afterward he cut green branches and threw them on to make smoke.

A long time seemed to pass. Ron put more wood and more branches on the fire. Surely someone would see the smoke. Suddenly he thought he heard a plane. Then he could see it. But it was miles off and flying away from him.

Then he heard another sound coming closer and closer. There it was—a helicopter coming right at him over the tops of the trees. He waved his arms. The helicopter floated to a landing on the grassy slope. Ron ran to it.

A ranger got out of the helicopter. "What's the idea of building a fire up here?" he demanded angrily.

"We need help. My father's hurt," Ron told him. He pointed. "He's down there in that gulch."

"Okay. We'll douse that fire, then take off."

They circled down the mountain and found a landing place near Ron's father.

The ranger examined him. "It's a broken leg, all right. And some bad bruises."

"How did you find us?" Ron's father asked.

When the ranger told him what Ron had done, his father smiled. "You've got plenty of courage, Ron. I'm lucky to have you with me."

Ron grinned. "But it's too bad you didn't get pictures of the weeping spruce, Dad."

"Weeping spruce," the ranger said. "You'll find two of them right up this gulch a little way. I want to put a splint on your father's leg before we lift him into the copter. There'll be plenty of time for you to take pictures of them, Ron."

Ron grabbed his father's camera. "I'll gather some of their cones, too."

"Thanks," called his father. "I'm glad you came along."

"Me, too," said Ron.

Victory for Jeff

By Miriam Graham

The starting whistle shrilled. From between the red buoys, fourteen small rowboats splashed forward. The Junior Dinghy Race was on.

Jeff had a wild moment when his boat, *River Rat*, fouled in a piece of underwater drift. He freed it with his right oar and was off a minute behind the others. For a twelve-year-old he had a good stroke. The long hours of practice were showing.

"Pull, two, three . . . pull, two, three," chanted Jeff. The eleven-foot *River Rat,* its white paint gleaming in the sun, spurted ahead. He passed the next three dinghies.

The water frothed as oars flashed and dipped into the green river. Like a family of ladybugs scattering toward home, the racers in their orange life jackets rocketed upstream toward the white finish buoy one mile ahead.

Steadily Jeff gained on the leaders. Soon there were only two boats to pass. In another five minutes there was one. Only Ed Winters was ahead.

"Don't count on it, Ed," Jeff muttered. "I'm coming."

Ed Winters had edged him out the last two years, coming in first for the trophy. Everyone who knew Ed had heard about it many times. This year Jeff had spared no effort to build muscle and staying power, for this would be his last race. The age limit was twelve.

Jeff pulled the *River Rat* toward the edge of the channel as he neared the inside curve of the river where the current was weakest. Here he could make better time. Today, though, a green runabout was in the way, crisscrossing as it explored the river. In it were a father, mother, and five children. Jeff worried when he saw how crowded the boat was.

Something else—no one, not even the smallest child, wore a life jacket!

Jeff had thought everyone knew that all small

children should wear life jackets on the water. His father, a coastguardsman, had taught him that adults, also, should wear jackets. He said regulations required a life jacket aboard for everyone in a boat.

Before Jeff could signal to the safety patrol boat running alongside the racers, the green runabout turned upstream and droned out of sight.

Jeff had lost time. He thought he heard oars splashing close behind. He dug his heels into the floorboards and pulled until his arms ached, driving toward the red victory flag waving from the tip of the white finish buoy. The splashing of the oars behind died away.

Stroke by stroke, grunt by grunt, Jeff gained on Ed Winters. Ed began to get nervous. Too many times he peeked over his shoulder. That slowed him down.

Jeff dug up an extra spurt of steam. He broke across Ed's wake, pulled alongside, and went by without looking at him. All he wanted to see was that red flag waving from the tip of the white finish buoy around the next bend.

He was fifteen feet in the lead and proud of himself as he rounded that last bend. What he saw there made him forget himself, Ed Winters, and the entire Junior Dinghy Race.

Fifty feet away the runabout, power lost, drifted as helpless as a leaf in an eddy. There was danger ahead. The green boat was in the path of a large wave which had been ploughed up by a passing cruiser.

The man in the green boat did his best to get his engine started so that he could head safely into the wave.

"Oh, no," groaned Jeff. The motor would not start.

To his alarm, the wave was traveling with the speed of an express train. He looked around and saw Ed Winters passing, going upstream. He screamed at him.

"Ed, boat in danger. Stand by."

Ed Winters did not look at him. He rowed steadily on toward the red victory flag.

It was scary how fast the wave approached. It caught the overloaded boat on the side, carrying it high into the air. The frightened passengers crowded to the other side. The boat, now off-balance, keeled over. Instantly, the whole family was in the water.

"Help!" cried the father. He caught the two youngest children in his arms and kicked to keep their heads above water.

"Help!" cried the mother, struggling to reach the other children.

"I'm coming," called Jeff. His oars flashed like propellers. "Keep kicking," he shouted. He saw the runabout's bottom surfacing as two of the older boys started to swim for shore. "Stay with the boat," he called. "It's coming up." At his call they turned back, heading for a handhold on the overturned runabout.

Jeff quartered his dinghy into the big wave when it hit, riding it easily. Soon he was at the scene, lifting the dripping toddlers into the *River Rat* and placing them low in his boat. When the others had been helped to firm handholds on the boats, Jeff reached under his seat for his horn and blew until his lips were numb.

Brrr...ooooo...ow—ow—OOOO!

Kuttt...kutt...kut, came an answer. It was the safety patrol boat. How good the chatter of its motor sounded to Jeff! It glided in with cut engines, closely followed by several small cruisers. Willing hands went to work, lifting the exhausted family aboard.

The safety patrol officer laid an arm over Jeff's shoulders. "Good boy, Jeff. We'll take over from here. Sorry about your race."

Jeff looked at him in surprise. He had forgotten the race. The red victory flag at the top of the white buoy had lost itself under the water together with the runabout. He sponged out the *River Rat* and headed for home.

Ed was back at the moorage showing his silver trophy when Jeff arrived. The miniature dinghy gleamed in the sun.

"Congratulations," said Jeff sincerely. "You have a good stroke."

"Same to you," said Ed. "I heard about the accident. They said you called, but I didn't hear you. Concentrating too hard, I guess. I thought you were still ahead."

Jeff believed him. Ed wasn't acting his usual triumphant self. He looked at Jeff in a way that was hard to understand. Anyone who didn't know Ed might think that he looked as if he thought Jeff was the one to come in first.

Ed wrapped his trophy in a piece of newspaper and put it in the corner of his bicycle basket. He hung one leg over the bar and stood for a moment digging in his pocket. When he found what he wanted, wadded and tightly rolled, he put it in Jeff's hand.

"Here," he said. "Here is something that belongs to you."

Jeff watched him pedal out of sight before he shook out the wad of cloth Ed had handed him. It was a red victory flag, streaked with a bit of white paint from the top of the finish buoy.

The Runaway Llama

By Mary Jane Biskupic

It was early morning, and Stacy couldn't believe what she saw trotting past her house. A shaggy-haired llama was in the middle of the street. It must have escaped from the zoo a mile away.

Stacy raced after the llama. A strap dangled from the animal's neck. Stacy tried to catch it. As she came closer, the frightened llama galloped faster.

Suddenly the llama stopped. The hanging strap had caught on a nail that was sticking out of a pole. The llama tried to free himself by running around the pole. This caused him to become tangled tight.

"Stay, boy, stay," said Stacy softly. She'd used those same words when she trained her dog, Rex, but they didn't work with the llama. The llama reared up and spit out a bad-smelling saliva.

"Take it easy," cried Stacy. "I'll get help." She ran to the corner phone booth and dialed 911. After she gave the operator all the information, she returned to the trapped llama.

Soon the sound of sirens was heard. The street filled with police cars and a large van from the zoo. A crowd gathered to watch what was happening. All this excitement frightened the llama even more. He spit out more bad-smelling saliva, and the crowd shrank back.

A man got out of the van from the zoo. Stacy ran up to him. "I hope you can help the llama," she said. "I didn't know calling the emergency number would bring such a crowd."

"Feliz is a frightened llama," said the zookeeper. "Llamas only spit when they are afraid. Nice boy, Feliz," said the zookeeper. He calmly stroked the llama's long shaggy hair. The llama stiffened his body.

"He doesn't look too happy," said Stacy.

The zookeeper carefully untangled the llama. Police officers held back the crowd as the zookeeper led the llama to the van. Stacy ran after him.

"May I visit Feliz at the zoo?" she asked.

"Come any time when the zoo is open," said the zookeeper. "Ask for me at the Children's Petting Zoo. My name is Tom Lang. You might be just what Feliz needs. The man who sold us the llama has a daughter your age. She named the llama Feliz. We thought Feliz would like living at our petting zoo, but we've even had trouble getting him to eat."

"I'll be there tomorrow, if my mom says it's all right," called Stacy as the van drove away.

The next day Stacy could hardly wait for the sun to come up. She was going to the zoo! But first she would stop at the library.

The librarian helped Stacy find two books that would help her learn some Spanish words. Stacy looked for words she might say to a llama if she were the girl who had raised him in South America. She said them over and over. Soon she felt ready to visit Feliz.

Mr. Lang recognized Stacy as she entered the petting zoo. "Since yesterday we've been keeping Feliz under tighter security. We still can't get him to eat anything. We're getting worried that he will become sick," Mr. Lang said.

Stacy looked at the llama sitting with his legs tucked under his body. He lay near a pile of hay in a small stall in the barn.

"I'd like to try to feed him," said Stacy. "Maybe

I could pretend to be the girl in South America. He might take some food from me."

"I don't want you too close until we know he has settled down," said Mr. Lang. "You can stand at the gate of his stall with this pan of water."

Stacy looked at the llama's long-lashed eyes and said good morning to him in Spanish. "*Buenos días.*"

The llama showed two front teeth but didn't move.

"I guess I wouldn't say 'Good morning' to a pet. I don't talk to Rex that way," Stacy said.

She thought for a minute, remembering how to say *water* in Spanish. "*Agua,*" said Stacy. "Here is *agua.*"

Slowly the llama unwrapped his legs and stood tall. For several minutes he stood looking at her.

"*Agua,*" said Stacy again. "*Beber.*"

Slowly Feliz clomped toward her. He sniffed at the pan of water. His long tongue stretched out and lapped up the water.

"*Bueno!*" Stacy stroked the llama's neck.

"Let's see if he will take some food from you," said Mr. Lang as he handed Stacy some green leaves.

She held out the greens to Feliz. The llama sniffed first, then took a dainty bite. After he had chewed the small piece for a long time, he swallowed and took another bite.

"You've helped us a lot," said Mr. Lang. "We

want you to come every day to help feed the llama."

"I wish there were some way that I could let the girl in South America know that her llama is all right," said Stacy.

"I'll get the address so that you can write to her," said Mr. Lang.

"Thanks. That will be great."

Soon after that Stacy had a pen pal named Carmen in South America. She also had a good friend named Feliz at the zoo.

Spanish Words in This Story

Happy
Feliz (fay-leez)

Good morning, good day
Buenos días
(bway-nohss dee-ahss)

Water
Agua (ah-gwah)

Good, happy
Bueno (bway-noh)

Drink
Beber (bay-bayr)

Lighthouse Vigil

By Jean Harmeling

"Robert! Joseph! Come look! The whales are back!" shouted Henry. Swelling with pride, he raced up the rocky path from the beach to his house overlooking the sea. What a lucky person he was! He could think of no other boy in the world who watched whales swim past his house, and it was not just any ordinary house either.

In the winter of 1872, Henry's father, Captain Robert Israel, had been assistant keeper for nearly a year at the Point Loma Lighthouse in San

Diego. It was one of the most important lighthouses on the Pacific Coast, guiding ships safely through the night. Henry's father had to take care that the powerful lamp in the tower was kept spotlessly clean and, most important, that its light burned brightly from sunset to sunrise.

Capt. Israel's job required a lot of responsibility. Henry was sure being a lighthouse keeper was the best job in the world. Other children might be lonely out on the cold, isolated point. But with the sea, Henry was never lonely. It brought abalone shells, starfish, ships, and, of course, the whales.

Henry dashed inside the lighthouse—a small, solid structure built of stone with its light tower sitting on top of the roof like a birthday candle. Henry found his two younger brothers and mother busy fixing breakfast in the kitchen.

"Mother! The whales are here! Where's Father? Robert, Joseph, come look!"

Mrs. Israel quickly wiped her hands. "Oh, your father's taken the wagon to town already with Uncle Enos. He'll be so disappointed."

The family hurried outside to the end of the point. In the swirling water below, they could see several large gray humps with white sprays shooting up from their spouts.

Robert and Joseph clapped their hands when they saw the giant creatures. Henry wished he could climb into his little fishing boat and follow them.

"Time to go back inside," his mother said soon. "It looks as if we're going to have some rain."

"Surely Father and Uncle Enos wouldn't have gone to town if it's going to rain," Henry said. "Besides, I don't think the sky looks rainy."

They trooped back inside for breakfast. Henry wished his father had not gone into town. But that was one of the problems of living far away in a lighthouse. Supplies and fresh water were not always available when they were needed.

Henry decided that he would go fishing that afternoon, but his mother's prediction came true. A little white cloud became a threatening gray one, bigger than the school of whales it hovered over. Soon there was rain everywhere, and the family huddled close to their stove for warmth.

"I hope Father gets home soon," Henry said, feeling worried. "It will be time to light the lamp."

Henry climbed the narrow spiral staircase to the top of the tower where the lamp waited to be lighted. He tried to catch sight of his father and Uncle Enos, but the rain lashed so hard against the windowpanes that his view of the point was only a muddled blur. Any chance of their returning from town in this storm seemed more and more hopeless.

After awhile Henry heard his mother's footsteps winding up around the stairs.

"Henry! We can't wait any longer for Father and Uncle Enos. We will have to light the lamp ourselves."

Henry hurried to open the lantern beneath the powerful lens. He was glad he had carefully watched his father light the wicks many times. With the oil all ready to burn, the lamp was not hard to light. In a moment, the flames of three wicks beamed through the magnifying lens almost as brilliantly as the sun.

Down below, Henry heard his little brother begin to cry. "Poor Mother," he said. "You have to worry about the whole family. I'll watch the light."

Mrs. Israel smiled wearily. "It's been a long day for us both, Henry. Let's hope Father and Uncle Enos get home safely."

As the hours slowly ticked by, Henry's eyes blinked and his head began to nod. But he knew he mustn't fall asleep.

"Henry, go to bed," his mother said as the rain finally began to clear from the window-panes. All was dark and still except for the beacon of light from the top of the tower.

Henry shook his head and rubbed his eyes. "I must watch the light, Mother. If it goes out, the sailors will be lost."

Just as Henry was sure he could no longer stay

awake, there was a sharp rapping at the door. Jumping to his feet, he raced down the stairs and flung it open. There stood his father and Uncle Enos, dripping wet and breathing heavily.

"Father! Uncle Enos! What happened to you?"

Capt. Israel sank weakly into a chair. "Our wagon broke down in town, and the storm was so bad the horse wouldn't go out in it. So we had to wait until the water was calm enough to row back."

Mrs. Israel threw her arms up in disbelief. "You rowed back? At night in this weather?"

Henry's father looked at his son with pride and understanding. "The lighthouse beacon was burning bright. We knew we would be safe."

Henry yawned. Now it was time to sleep.

Thanks to Mary

By Ann Bixby Herold

When Mary first saw the men, she was afraid. They looked desperate enough for anything. It was just before nightfall, and Mary was returning to the farm where she worked. As the three men came toward her along the path, she wrapped her brown cloak around herself and dived for cover.

Hidden in a thicket, she breathed a sigh of relief. They hadn't seen her.

As they passed by, Mary could see they were

so tired that they stumbled.

"I'm hungry," groaned one. "I'd give anything for a bowl of my wife's good soup."

"We're all hungry, John." The next man sighed. He walked with a limp.

"It's my Betsy's tenth birthday next month." The third man spoke in a low, sad voice. "I promised her I'd be done with soldiering and be home by then."

Soldiers!

Mary stayed extra still. Ragged and shivering with cold, the men looked more like beggars. They were from the encampment at Valley Forge, Mary guessed. She had heard about them from the Lewis family, the people she worked for.

"Stay clear of the encampment, Mary," Mrs. Lewis had warned her. "Those rebels are dangerous."

They certainly *look* dangerous, Mary thought. But they don't *sound* dangerous. Just tired and hungry and sad.

Slowly, her cold fingers slid into her skirt pockets. There, still warm from the oven, were two round oatcakes Mrs. Lewis had given her for delivering a message. There were three soldiers, but two oatcakes were better than none. Mary pushed her way out of the bushes and ran after the men.

"Wait!" she called.

They spun around. Their faces were tense.

They relaxed when they saw the small girl.

"Why lookee here," cried the man with the limp. "Have we strayed into slave country?"

"I'm no slave!" Mary's eyes flashed. "I'm free born, same as you."

"He didn't mean anything by it," said the man with the daughter called Betsy. "He's too hungry to think straight."

Mary relaxed and held out the oatcakes. "I brought you these. You'll have to share. Two is all I have."

The men stared at the fragrant oatcakes as if they couldn't believe their eyes.

"Take them." Mary thrust them at the men. "I have to go now. If I'm not back at the farm by dark, there will be trouble."

"Wait," the men cried. "Who are you? We want to thank you."

But Mary McDonald was on her way.

That night, warm and snug in her small cot up in the attic, Mary thought about the hungry soldiers. She knew that Mr. Lewis sent vegetables and grain by the wagonload to the markets in British-occupied Philadelphia. Why didn't he sell some to General Washington at nearby Valley Forge?

The next morning she asked Mrs. Lewis.

"Because the British pay with good money," her mistress snapped. "The rebels give us nothing but empty promises."

"But . . . ," said Mary.

"It's none of your business, Mary. Why aren't those dishes done?"

Mary sighed. She couldn't forget the look on the soldiers' faces when they saw the fresh-baked oatcakes.

Every time she sat down to a meal, she thought about the soldiers. She had plenty to eat, and they were starving. She had warm clothes to wear, and they were aching with cold in their ragged uniforms. It bothered her more and more.

She started to save some of her food—some nuts here, an apple there.

When her basket was full, she bundled up her few belongings. Early one morning, while the Lewis family was still asleep, she let herself out of the house.

It was a bitter cold morning. At Valley Forge the shivering sentry on lookout duty let her pass. When she reached General Washington's headquarters, she knocked at the door.

"I'm Mary McDonald. I've come to join the army," she told Washington's startled sentry.

"You? Girls can't join the army."

"I've brought some food." Mary handed him an apple.

The sentry grinned down at her. "Follow me, ma'am," he said. He took her to Mrs. Washington.

"Mary McDonald is here to join the army, ma'am," he announced.

Mrs. Washington smiled. "We have need of busy hands," she said.

There was plenty of work to do. Mary sewed. She knitted. She carried baskets of food and other comforts to the sick soldiers in their cabins.

Mary knew the countryside well. She ran messages to homes sympathetic to the rebel army. No one ever stopped or questioned her. She could go places a grown-up would not dare.

Hurrying along an icy path early one morning, Mary's sharp eyes saw something perched high in a clump of trees. It was a man dressed all in brown. He was staring out over the encampment.

It seemed he hadn't seen Mary, so she doubled back for a closer look. She moved up the hill from tree to tree. She was careful to walk only on the bare patches that matched her brown cloak.

The man had a telescope. He was staring through it and writing in a notebook. He looked well fed and warmly dressed. Mary was sure he didn't come from Valley Forge.

A spy! she thought.

Silently she crept away. When she reached the path, she slipped on the ice and fell. The man looked down the hill toward her. Then he turned away. Why would he suspect a young girl?

The officer on duty at Valley Forge sent four soldiers back with Mary. The man was too busy spying on the encampment to notice them making their way up the hill. The soldiers made Mary hide behind a rock while they captured him.

The man was a British spy sent from Philadelphia. With his capture Mary became a hero. The officers in camp all raised their hats when Mary walked by. The sentries saluted her.

Someone even heard General Washington say, "If I had more soldiers like Mary McDonald, this war would be won by now."

● ●

This is a made-up story, but it is based on fact. General Washington's army did camp at Valley Forge in the winter of 1777-1778, and they were short of food and clothing. Martha Washington spent much of the winter with her husband. She and other women at the camp tried to make the soldiers' lives easier by patching uniforms, preparing food baskets, and tending the sick.

Tomik to the Rescue

By Kay Jones

Tomik quickly pulled on his caribou-skin parka.

His mother, who was straightening the fur rugs on the sleeping platform, glanced up. "Are you going out to feed the dogs?"

Tomik nodded and tightened the rawhide thongs on his long boots.

"When Father gets home from the seal hunt, he'll be proud to hear how well you have cared for his team," said Mother, smiling.

"I hope Father will be home soon," put in Tomik's little brother. "It's been a long time since he went off across the sea ice in Grandfather's big sledge. I miss him."

"Chimo misses him, too," declared Tomik. "He's the only one of Father's dogs who is still sad and unfriendly."

"Ee—eee, I'm afraid of Chimo!" his brother exclaimed. "Those big, fierce eyes and sharp teeth make me want to run and run. Aren't you afraid of him, Tomik?"

Tomik flushed. "Sometimes," he muttered, ashamed of admitting his fear of the dog.

"Why is he Father's favorite?"

"Because he's such a good lead dog," said Tomik as he headed outside. "He's led our team home safely through many great blizzards."

When Tomik emerged from the round-topped igloo of earth and rock, he took some chunks of frozen seal meat out of a food cache nearby and crossed the hard-packed snow to the place where the huskies were tied. At the sight of their dinner the animals strained forward in eager anticipation, their big bushy tails waving a welcome. After they had devoured every last morsel, Tomik went among them to stroke the tawny heads with gentle hands. All but Chimo responded affectionately. Whenever Tomik approached him, he would growl deep in his throat and edge away.

He seemed to sense Tomik's fear of him.

A short time later Tomik returned to the igloo, bent down, and stepped through the low doorway. But when he was less than halfway along the tunnel, he heard a sudden commotion of yaps and howls from the dogs. Turning back, he rushed outside again to see what was the matter.

The moment he reached them, he saw that one was missing. Chimo had slipped his collar. Why had Chimo broken loose? And what would Father say if he came home to find his team without a leader? He had to find Chimo!

Tomik quieted the excited dogs, and it was then that he heard another one in the distance. Chimo! He started forward, rushed back to get Chimo's collar, and raced off again. After going along a narrow trail for a few minutes, he veered to the left and headed toward a towering, ice-caked boulder jutting up from a small hill. As he drew closer to it, fear stabbed him as he heard the menacing growls coming from the far side. Was Chimo growling at him, he wondered, or for some other reason?

Tomik slowed his steps and tightened his mittened fingers about the dog's heavy collar. Then he scrambled up the snowy hill to the boulder and peered around the edge. The hill dropped sharply to a small hollow, strewn with jagged rocks. In the center of the hollow crouched

Chimo, teeth bared in a snarl, yellow eyes glaring straight ahead. Relieved not to be the focus of the dog's fury, Tomik craned his neck farther, then ducked back with a shiver.

Nanook! Now he knew what had caused the team's wild excitement—the scent of polar bear! The huge animal was standing about fifteen feet away, swinging its massive head angrily to and fro.

With pounding heart Tomik again poked his head around the boulder. Why was Chimo crouched in that awkward position? Why wasn't he attacking Nanook? He leaned forward for a closer view and immediately saw that one of Chimo's hind legs was caught between the rocks. Right then the bear started lumbering toward the helpless dog.

For an instant, Tomik froze. He knew that a single sweep of a polar bear's gigantic paw had knocked many an attacking husky unconscious. But what would happen to a trapped one? He shuddered and wished he were old enough to carry a rifle. He must somehow get Nanook's attention away from Chimo.

Just as the bear was about to lunge, Tomik suddenly straightened up, raised his arm, and with all his strength hurled Chimo's collar. It hit the side of the huge animal's head sharply, taking the bear by surprise. The collar fell to the ground with a thud.

Hardly daring to breathe, Tomik watched the bear come to a halt, lift its head slowly, and sniff the air. Does he smell me? Tomik wondered uneasily. After a long moment (it seemed forever to Tomik), the animal turned and without a backward glance at the dog, lumbered off.

Tomik went limp with relief, then instantly stiffened again. The bear had come to a halt about thirty feet away and was once more sniffing the air and wagging his head back and forth suspiciously.

That was when Tomik decided to act. This moment might be the only chance to free Chimo from the rocks. Suppressing his fear of the dog, he half-slid, half-fell down the hill. When Chimo saw him, he continued to glare and growl but permitted Tomik to kneel by his side. He seemed to know that Tomik wanted to help. With swift fingers he loosened the sharp rocks trapping Chimo's leg. Then, grasping the dog's rough coat tightly so he wouldn't try to attack the bear, Tomik hauled him up toward the protecting boulder.

After they were safely behind it, Tomik peered around the edge cautiously and saw that Nanook was once again on the move. He watched until the bear reached the shoreline. When it finally disappeared from sight, a wave of relief swept through the young boy.

It was then that Tomik suddenly felt a cold, wet nose nudge his cheek. He turned and gazed directly into the furry face of Chimo. The dog's yellow eyes no longer glared. They were regarding him with warmth and affection. That was when Tomik knew he had made a friend.

Rogue Elephant

By Marlene Richardson

The Indian sun was hot and high in the heavens when Ranjit heard the crashing of branches. Instinctively he jumped out of the way, just in time! The big gray form was a blur as it stormed through the jungle, trumpeting in anger. It took a few seconds for the boy to realize that it was Cheeni, the elephant for whom he had been searching all morning. But it was a Cheeni that was behaving wild and strange, not like the elephant that Ranjit had played with as far back as he could remember. The elephant then had such a sweet, gentle nature that he had been named "Cheeni," the native word meaning sugar.

"Cheeni, Cheeni, come here, come here!" called Ranjit.

The elephant acted as if he hadn't heard or seen Ranjit and thundered out of sight, uprooting everything in his path. Puzzled and bewildered, Ranjit headed for the village as fast as he could. Father will know what's wrong, he thought. He knows more about elephants than anyone! After all, he is the number one *mahout* in the village and has trained and worked with more elephants hauling teak logs in the jungles than anyone else.

"Father, Father," yelled Ranjit. "I found Cheeni, but he acted so wild and angry I hardly knew him."

"Wild and angry? What do you mean?" asked his father.

Ranjit told his father exactly how Cheeni had behaved, and with every word his father's face became more serious.

"What is it, Father?" asked Ranjit. "What's the matter with Cheeni?"

"I'm sorry, Ranjit, but it sounds as if Cheeni has turned into a rogue elephant. I will have to tell the District Officer, because if it is true, he will have to be shot."

"Shoot him? Shoot Cheeni?" cried Ranjit. "But why?"

"I'm sorry, my son," said his father. "But a rogue elephant is an elephant gone crazy and in his anger destroys everything in sight."

"Oh, Father," pleaded Ranjit. "Don't tell them about Cheeni! I know he wouldn't do anything bad, and I love him so much."

"Ranjit, I know how much you love Cheeni," said his father. "Have I not seen you share every sweet and piece of sugarcane with him? Have I not heard all the villagers remark that never have they seen such love between elephant and boy? But if Cheeni is a rogue, he is very dangerous. I must tell the District Officer."

Ranjit's father reported Cheeni's behavior to the District Officer, who had already received reports of a rogue elephant on the loose.

"I never thought it could be Cheeni!" said the surprised District Officer. "Vegetable plots and banana groves have been torn up, even two villagers' huts were destroyed, but no one has been hurt. Tomorrow we will look for him and shoot on sight."

When Ranjit heard what the District Officer had said, he burst into tears. There was no consoling him. He went to bed without eating, but his sleep was filled with dreams of rogue elephants.

Ranjit awoke in the middle of the night, his

heart pounding. He knew what he must do. He must find Cheeni first. He would never forget his best friend, even if he was a rogue.

Ranjit knew exactly where he would go, a wild sugarcane field where Cheeni often went. Ranjit arrived there before sunrise and settled down under a tree. He didn't have long to wait. He heard Cheeni long before he saw him, and judging from the noise, he was as angry as ever! Ranjit quickly clambered up to the highest branch. He was very frightened, but he was determined to save his friend.

"Cheeni, Cheeni," called Ranjit. "Don't you remember me? I'm your friend, Ranjit. Please don't act this way, Cheeni, or they will have to shoot you!"

The elephant listened, flapping his ears, and for a minute Ranjit thought he understood. But no, the elephant raised his trunk, sniffed the air, and, then trumpeting, angrily charged the tree.

Ranjit hung on desperately, wishing he hadn't come out alone. This was a Cheeni he didn't know! As he looked down on the lowered head of Cheeni, his eyes caught sight of a terrible wound behind his ear. He couldn't be sure but it looked like a bullet wound.

"Oh, Cheeni, my poor Cheeni, somebody has shot you!" cried Ranjit. "Please let me help you!"

It was in that instant the sound of a shot rang out. Luckily it just missed Cheeni! In the distance

Ranjit could see two men with raised rifles. They would shoot again if he didn't do something.

Wildly waving one free arm in the air, Ranjit loudly shouted, "Don't shoot! Don't shoot! Cheeni has been hurt. He's not a rogue! Don't shoot!"

The District Officer heard Ranjit's cries, and as he was also responsible for the safety of the wildlife, he always carried a tranquilizing gun which he now quickly loaded with a double dose, enough for such a big animal. He fired into Cheeni's flank, and in a few seconds the elephant was dazed and staggering on his big legs.

The District Officer worked quickly to remove the bullet that was lodged in the bone behind Cheeni's ear.

"Some ivory poacher must have shot him," said the District Officer. "With that pain, no wonder he acted like a rogue! Don't worry, Ranjit, when he wakes up in a couple of hours he'll be as good as new."

For two hours Ranjit waited on the edge of the village, and his heart leaped with joy when in the distance he saw his Cheeni ambling home, gently swaying his trunk, looking for sweet twigs and branches. Yes, it was the old Cheeni—thanks to the devotion of his friend, Ranjit.

The Captive

By Lois Breitmeyer and Gladys Leithauser

Josie Turner scrambled down the mountain trail from her house to the valley. She couldn't be late for her first real job!

Although early morning mist half hid the valley, she could see the big sign that marked her destination—SAM'S SERVICE STATION: FAST FUEL AND FOOD.

Then Josie saw something move outside the building. It looks like an animal inside a cage, she thought as she started to run.

But investigating had to wait. Sam Dickson was

standing at the station door.

"Hello. I'm glad you're here!" Josie's new employer tapped the walking cast on his left leg. "This broken ankle makes working mighty hard. I can use your help."

The morning was busy. Wiping windshields, making sandwiches, bringing soda pop, Josie forgot the motion she had seen in the fog—until eleven o'clock, when she ran around the building. In a cage a large eagle ruffled his bronze feathers and cocked his head as Josie approached.

Mr. Dickson hobbled up. "Isn't he a beauty? Found him—hurt. But he's well now."

"First one I've ever seen," Josie said.

"How'd you like to take over feeding him?"

"Yes, sir! But isn't keeping an eagle against the law? Why don't you let him go?"

"Let him go!" Mr. Dickson echoed. "Why, I saved his life. Besides, I like him."

Later Josie carried out a tray of meat scraps. She slid it into the cage. "Here, old fellow."

The eagle's strong beak tore into the meat scraps, and soon the tray was empty. Josie stared uncomfortably as the bird pushed his wings fiercely against the cage. "If you were free," Josie declared, "you could find your own dinner."

Josie loved her new job. Only one thing bothered her—the eagle. Somehow it seemed wrong for such a splendid wild creature to be trapped.

"I've been reading about wild birds," she said one afternoon when Mr. Dickson was resting his leg. "Did you know eagles keep the same nest year after year?" She glanced at her employer. "Bet your eagle's thinking about his home right now."

"Nonsense," Sam Dickson said sharply. "That bird has a good home right here."

"I guess so," Josie murmured, afraid to say more.

When she arrived the next morning, heavy clouds were gathering overhead. Josie knew they signaled a big storm.

"Maybe you should wait until tomorrow to go for supplies," she said to Mr. Dickson, who was writing a list.

"Nope. I always go Tuesdays. Don't worry. I'll be fine." Sam Dickson climbed awkwardly into his red pickup truck.

"Don't forget the bread," Josie called as the truck pulled away. Before it disappeared, thunder sounded, and a downpour began.

Only one customer appeared all morning. "Roads are bad," the driver declared. "Hope this rain stops before we have a mudslide."

By noon Josie was worried. Mr. Dickson should have been back by this time. "I'll call town," she said. She picked up the telephone; it was dead. "The lines are down! I'd better look for him."

Pulling on her slicker, Josie walked along the deserted, rain-washed road. She wondered where the cars were. She started to run, turned a bend in the road . . . then she saw it—a great pile of rocks, upside-down trees, twisted roots holding chunks of earth.

"A mudslide! The road's blocked! What if Mr. Dickson was coming back and . . ."

Slipping, struggling, Josie climbed on a huge rock and began to shout, "Mr. Dickson!" She searched the jumble of mud, rocks, and branches. She shouted again, "Mr. Dickson! Mr. . . ."

Wait! Was that a patch of red? The truck? Quickly, she pushed her way through broken trees until she was certain.

Moments later, hands and face scratched, she reached the truck. It lay on its side, pinned down by a giant tree, and the exposed door was smashed in. Josie could hear Mr. Dickson pounding and yelling.

"I'm trapped!" Mr. Dickson cried. "Get me out."

Josie tugged at the buckled door. "It won't budge," she shouted. "I'll get help!"

It was a long trip to town, but Josie ran the whole way. When she stumbled into the sheriff's office, she was so breathless she could hardly speak.

"Trapped!" exclaimed Sheriff Jones when Josie finally made herself understood. He grabbed a first-aid kit and a crowbar. "Let's go!"

Bouncing along in the sheriff's jeep, Josie pointed the way to the red truck. The two jumped out, yelling as they scrambled through tree branches.

"We're here, Mr. Dickson!"

"Hang on, Sam!"

He wedged the crowbar between the truck body and the buckled door. Then he took a firm hold on the thick handle.

"Help pull! Hard!" the sheriff shouted to Josie. The door didn't move. "Harder!"

With a loud, crunching noise, the door broke open. Josie and the sheriff half dragged the frightened man from the truck. Then the three drove along back roads to the service station.

Josie helped Mr. Dickson inside and started toward the kitchen. "You need some hot soup."

"Thank you, Josie. Now I want to do something for you."

Josie hesitated. "There *is* something. I know the best reward. . . ."

Mr. Dickson stared at her. "The eagle?"

She nodded.

"You want to turn him loose, don't you?"

"Yes, sir."

Sam Dickson half smiled. "I do, too. Now I know how it feels to be trapped. Go ahead. Open the cage."

Outside, the rain had stopped. Josie unlatched the cage door and swung it open. The eagle gazed solemnly at the man and girl. Then he stepped out onto the platform.

Suddenly he sprang! Strong wings spread wide, then beat more and more powerfully to lift him to freedom. The eagle, no longer captive, soared into the afternoon sky.

Juan Ramos
and the Great White Shark

By Al Eason

Juan Ramos, his body gleaming with the wetness of the sea, had no inkling of danger as he waded into the clear water with the new cast net. A coral boulder had gashed his leg as he hurried toward the surfacing school of anchovies, and now the wound was stinging from the salt water. Excited by the mass of fish, he disregarded the wound.

Unknown to Juan, a faint trail of blood was washed along with the ebbing tide. Far out over the multihued coral reef, a great white shark turned and began following the tantalizing scent of the blood.

Unsuspecting, Juan flung the cast net. The cast was fair—as well as his father could do—and Juan saw the muted flashes of thousands of tiny shapes as the weighted outer edge of the circular net settled around the trapped fish. Juan was jubilant. With such success he could buy the sewing machine for Mama!

If life was hard on Sibuyan, Juan was not aware of the hardships. The island with its 6,750-foot mountain peak, located in the midst of the Philippines, was an exciting place for a boy. Had Juan's life not been filled with fishing? Was he not following the way of his father and grandfathers? Juan was happy. His ambition was to become as good a fisherman as his father and to earn enough money to buy his mother a sewing machine. Juan had seven brothers and sisters. His mother needed the machine for her business. Only Juanita, his twin sister, was old enough to help with the project.

As Juan dived to gather the lead line of the net, Juanita pulled the *banka* clear of the beach. She climbed agilely into the dugout, ready to assist her brother with the catch of fish. Juanita was dark-haired and pretty. She was also a good fisherman.

Juan surfaced with a shout. "Hey, Juanita, come

quick! The net is loaded with fish!" He gathered the weighted lines over a shoulder and began struggling toward the *banka*. Juanita paddled swiftly to his aid.

Juan reached the boat and quickly lashed the lines of the net to the bamboo outrigger. Now he could pull both boat and net while Juanita paddled. They had begun making slight headway when the first mackerel streaked by the boat.

"Look! Look!" Juan exclaimed. "They are going straight to the trap." He pointed excitedly. An endless stream of fish were entering the trap. It was constructed of a series of V-shaped palm mats, held in place by posts. As the tide receded, the fish would be caught in points of the V's.

Juanita was excited, too. Standing in the *banka*, she was nearly thrown overboard when an onslaught of larger fish struck the boat.

Juan vaulted aboard with a worried look on his face.

"What's wrong?" Juanita's dark eyes were questioning.

"Tuna," Juan replied, seeming puzzled. "The fish around the boat are tuna. They belong in blue water. I've never seen one over the reef before."

"Are we in danger?"

"Not from the tuna. But wait a minute! First the anchovies, then mackerel, tuna, and—yes! Yes, of course! Next will come the barracudas and sharks. This is the cycle of the sea. We must get to the beach before the sharks come!" As his brown eyes swept seaward, they widened in disbelief.

The smaller fish were not feeding. They were fleeing in abject terror from a mammoth shark! Less than fifty yards away, Juan could see the triangular dorsal fin slicing through the dark mass of leaping tuna. The shark was on a course straight for the boat!

Perhaps the shark will swerve, and I can save the fish in the net, Juan thought. The anchovies would provide enough additional money to buy the machine. But no! I must think of Juanita's safety. To delay would be foolish and dangerous. Quickly he drew his sheath knife and cut the net free.

Released from the encumbering net, the *banka* was easier to handle. The twins drove it toward the beach with rapid strokes of the paddles.

They had abandoned the net not a second too soon. With cavernous mouth agape, the huge shark surged into the cast net. A second later its tremendous body rose clear of the water and fell back with a resounding splash.

Clinging remnants of the net shrouded the great head and eyes. Torn portions of the net trailed from the shark's gill slits. Choking and blinded by the stout webbing, the shark went berserk.

A long curving run carried the wildly thrashing shark between the twins and the safety of the beach. Although half-aground, the twenty-five-foot length of the shark formed an effective barrier to their escape.

"What shall we do?" Juan cried.

"There is only one safe place," said Juanita. "We must reach the trap. Paddle as fast as you can!"

Juan dug his oar into the water, but he was not sure even the trap would hold the awesome power of the shark.

They reached the outer V of the trap only moments before the shark swam free of the beach. As the twins huddled behind the doubtful safety of the posts, the blinded shark plowed into the sections of the trap near the beach. Its huge weight sheared the small posts of the trap as easily as toothpicks, scattering fish, and dragging whole segments of the trap seaward.

The shark seemed to sense that escape lay toward deeper waters. With renewed power, it bludgeoned through successive V's of the trap, gathering additional posts and palm matting.

The twins waited, scarcely breathing. Only three more V's of the trap separated them from the shark.

"He seems to be weakening," Juan whispered hopefully. The last butting charge of the shark had been thrown back by the posts.

Now the ebb tide was at full flow.

"Do you really think so, Juan?"

"Yes," Juan replied, putting his arm around his sister. "These last posts are larger and are set in coral. When Father and I built this section, we used the trunks of black palm. No stronger wood grows on all of Sibuyan. Yes, I believe the trap will hold."

Juan was right. The mass of trailing material and added size of the posts had proved too much for the shark. The springy resilience of the stout palm logs defied a last feeble effort, leaving the shark stranded amid a great mass of choice fish.

The tide was out—the excitement over.

As they surveyed the litter of flopping fish, the twins overflowed with relief and high spirits.

"Hurry, Sister," Juan said. "Hurry to the *barrio* and tell everyone to come quickly with baskets. We have enough fish for the whole island!"

She paused and turned with a questioning look. "And enough for Mama's sewing machine?"

"Enough for two machines for Mama." Juan grinned.

Juanita returned the grin and raced down the beach to spread the good news.

The Stranger

By Arnold A. Griese

The April sun had already climbed over the top of the tall spruce trees along the high bank of the Yukon River. It shone down on a thick blanket of snow brought in by yesterday's late winter storm. And it shone down on two children as they struggled through the deep snow which covered the trail to their rabbit snares.

Girl, the older, pushed back the hood on her fur parka as she knelt down and carefully dug away the snow from the last snare on their trapline. It was empty—like all the rest.

Girl's little brother knelt beside her and looked down at the empty snare. Trying hard to hide his tears, he said, "Again, today, there will be nothing to eat."

"Today, Little One, Older Brother or one of the other men might come back from the mountains carrying a caribou. Then the whole village will eat." Girl said this only to make him feel better. She knew the caribou were gone from the hills.

Girl stood up, brushed the wet snow from her knees, smiled down at Little One, and said, "Remember, soon the ice will leave the river, and then many salmon will come upstream to feed us."

Little One stood up, too. Girl took his hand and led him off the trail to the riverbank as she said, "Now we will let the sun warm us as we rest."

They sat, saying nothing. Little One closed his eyes, but Girl looked downriver. Her thoughts were on the strangers. They had already visited the villages to the south, and all winter there had been talk of their coming here. Everyone feared these strangers. Some said they carried long sticks that made a sound like thunder and killed from far away. Others said they came from under the ground, from the land of the dead where there was no sun or wind to make their skin brown like that of the Indians. Many thought they had seen these strangers coming. And just this morning Girl's mother had warned her to be careful and to be on the lookout for them.

Slowly these thoughts faded as the warm sun, her hunger, and the work of breaking trail through the snow made her sleepy.

Then a sudden sound woke Girl, and she looked around. Below, along the river's edge and not far away, a man struggled through the snow.

Quickly Girl put her hand over Little One's mouth. When his eyes opened, she motioned for him to move with her, back behind a tree. From there she watched as Little One asked, "What is it?"

"A man," Girl answered.

"Is he one of ours?"

Without looking away, she said, "No, he walks differently."

Little One whispered, "Then it is one of the strangers. We must go!"

Girl turned her head as she said, "We cannot be sure. We must let him come closer. Our trail is broken. We will easily reach the village before he does."

Little One was afraid now and pressed up against Girl as she watched. Just then two spruce hens flew by and started across the river. The man pointed a long stick at them, a loud noise echoed through the trees, and both birds fell dead alongside the river.

Little One grabbed Girl's arm as she turned to go. She stopped to give one last look. "He goes for the birds, and new snow covers the many holes at the river's edge," she whispered.

For a moment they stood looking. Little One spoke first. "It will be better for our people if he falls in the river."

Yes, it would be better for our people, Girl thought; but then she said, "He does not know of the danger. We do."

Again, Girl turned to watch. She still did not know what to do.

Now the man had reached the birds and was putting them into his parka pockets. Maybe he will get away from the ice safely, she thought.

But he didn't. Suddenly, he fell through, and she saw only his head and hands.

And, just as suddenly, Girl acted. She called out to Little One, "Wait here and watch. If the stranger does not let me come back, run quickly and tell Mother!" She then plunged down the steep bank to the river. As she struggled on, she looked for and found a long spruce pole. Wrenching it out of the snowbank, she moved carefully along the ice, holding the pole straight across in front of her. It would hold her up if the ice gave way.

When Girl was close enough, she pushed the pole out toward the stranger. It was then that he turned his head and saw her.

For a moment, when Girl first saw his face, she felt fear. The face she saw was twisted and its huge eyes stared at her. Suddenly she knew it for the look of terror, his eyes wide in panic.

She forgot her fear as she saw his bare hands slipping and clawing at the ice. Quickly she pushed the pole closer. He grabbed it with both hands. As Girl braced against a block of ice and held on to the other end, the stranger climbed out of the water. Then he grabbed the pole with one hand and Girl's arm with the other and hurried onto the bank.

Once they were safe, he let go of Girl's arm, and she thought about running away to Little One. Instead, she looked up into his strange face. This time she saw only the smile he gave her as he reached into his parka pockets, pulled out the two spruce hens, and handed them to her.

Girl gave him a shy smile as she took the birds. Then a worried look crossed her face as she saw his wet clothes. She pointed to his clothes, to herself, and then to her village. He nodded to show that he understood and turned to get his pack.

As Girl watched him pick up his stick-that-kills, she no longer feared the stranger. Now she knew she had done right.

• •

This is not a true story but it is based on actual facts. In 1838 the Athabascan Indians of Alaska met Russian explorers, the first white people they had ever seen.

Anna's Rescue Signal

By Robert and Amy Cloud

Anna Bergen stood on the dock of tiny Bergen Island and watched her father and older brother Arne chug out of sight in the family motorboat. She wished she were older. Nothing exciting ever happened to a ten-year-old. Instead of going off overnight in the boat, she had to stay home and help Mom. She sighed.

When the tractor had stopped working, her dad quickly discovered the broken part. "We'll have to head to the big machine shops to get this part fixed. If we catch all tides right, we should be back tomorrow," he'd said.

Now Anna and her mother were alone on the small island where her family had farmed the forty acres for generations.

Anna was glad she lived now, instead of long ago. At least now we have the radio, she thought, and the motorboat. And the Coast Guard helicopter comes over twice a day. All we need is a telephone, and we'd be as modern as city folks.

Her mother was calling, and Anna climbed the slight rise toward the house. Her mother had the family washing well under way. Anna helped sort the clothing into piles—whites and colors, cottons and permanent press—while her mother operated the washer.

The morning was nearly gone, and Anna kept an ear and eye toward the sky. She always liked to watch for the Coast Guard helicopter and wave at the pilot. He flew south over the island every day just before noon and returned an hour later on his way back to home base on Thursday Island. He would dip to 300 feet and circle the house before going on.

Often the Bergen wash would already be on the line—a long double wire on pulleys from a post near the porch to the top of a forty-foot pine —when the copter pilot came by.

"That washline looks just like the pennant line

on the admiral's flagship," the pilot once told Anna and her dad when the three met in Thursday Harbor.

Anna had hung the first load of wash when she heard the helicopter's familiar *chut-chut-chut* approach, then fade away.

She started out with the next load, but the full basket bumped her knees.

"Here, Anna," her mother said, "I'll take it out for you." She picked up the heavy basket and carried it to the door.

As she started down the porch steps, her heel caught on a board, and in an instant she was flat on the hard ground. The basket of clothes partially broke her fall, but she landed heavily on one hip.

"Anna! Anna!" she cried. "Help! I can't get up."

Anna leaped down the steps to her mother and pulled the clothes basket away. She knelt on the ground and anxiously held her mother's hand.

"Can we get you in the house, Mommy? If we could get you into a warm bed, then we could have Daddy . . ." Her voice trailed off as she remembered her father and Arne were both gone. She would have to help her mother, get help from outside. But how? No island was near enough to signal.

Her mother struggled to sit up but could not.

"Anna, I think it's my leg. I must lie here till help comes. Can you find something warm to put around me?"

Anna rushed into the house and returned with an armful of blankets. She carefully tucked them around her mother. Her mind was racing. The Coast Guard! The copter was due back within the hour. Could she get the pilot's attention?

She had a hopeful thought. Did she dare tell her mother—perhaps give her false hope if the idea failed?

She quickly picked out the brightest colored clothing she could find. She started spreading them on the grass in a giant SOS.

Her mother was watching from where she lay by the porch. "Anna, what are you doing?"

"Sending a message, Mommy. I'll wash these again. I promise."

Her mother smiled at that, though her eyes showed pain. "I'm afraid you'll have to do all the laundry for awhile, Anna. I won't be able to do much."

Anna finished her message with shirts and dresses. Would the copter pilot see it? She scanned the sky. Suddenly her anxious ears picked up the helicopter's *chut-chut-chut* returning from the south.

Swiftly she picked up a red-and-yellow dress she had placed aside and ran back and forth across the yard waving it. The copter pilot dipped low and circled slowly. She could see him leaning across and looking at her.

She darted back and forth, shouting, "Help! Help!" But she could not shout above the copter's noise. She stopped beside her mother and flapped the dress vigorously. The pilot studied the ground, then looked back to Anna, as his copter circled.

Then the machine suddenly tilted up on edge and sped rapidly northward. Had he read her message? Did he understand? All Anna could do now was wait.

She sat by her mother for what seemed like hours. But it was really less than one hour when suddenly from the north came a big helicopter, twice the size of the Coast Guard patrol machine. It flew straight to their island, circled, then settled on a clearing behind the house. In a moment, two men in white Coast Guard medical uniforms came running, carrying a stretcher.

They spoke softly to Mrs. Bergen, then gently moved her to the stretcher and carried it to the waiting helicopter. Anna walked alongside.

"Leave a note for your father," Mrs. Bergen told Anna. "Tell him we'll be at the hospital in Thursday Harbor. The Coast Guard will let us know when he returns."

After Anna had placed the note on the kitchen

table, she tossed her wash-day SOS in a basket. Then she ran back to the copter. The men helped her inside. With a great whirring of the blades, the big machine rose. The house got smaller and smaller; soon the whole island was in sight.

As the helicopter swung north and started its run to the hospital, Anna found her mother's hand and squeezed. Her mother squeezed back and drew Anna down to her. "The men told me, Anna, that what you did showed quick thinking." She smiled. "They said you are a real heroine."

First Flight

By Josephine Bell

Early morning light peeked through the venetian blinds into Nick's bedroom. It was Saturday, the day he'd been dreading all week. His Uncle Tony had invited him to help fly much-needed supplies to the fishermen on Kodiak Island, a large island south of mainland Alaska.

Most boys would have been excited, but not Nick. He had promised to go only to keep his sister and friends from calling him a sissy. Besides, he didn't want to disappoint his uncle. Other than his own family, Uncle Tony was his most favorite person in the whole world. Not many boys had an Alaskan bush pilot for an uncle.

Bush pilots flew in both fair and stormy weather, carrying food and medicine to isolated villages. When anyone was injured or in trouble, pilots also flew to their rescue. Nick admired the pilots, but he was afraid to fly.

Brrr, brrr sounded the alarm clock. Nick groaned and pulled the blanket over his face. Then he heard his father's footsteps coming down the hall.

"Rise and shine, Nick. It's time to leave for the airfield. Uncle Tony will be waiting."

It was too late now. He had to go. "Coming, Dad," Nick called as he scrambled out of bed. He hurried into his clothes. As he started to tie his shoes, he heard his sister Susie and his parents laughing and talking at the breakfast table. They were happy for him. He didn't want to disappoint them, so he tried to look excited as he ran to the kitchen.

Nick ate his scrambled eggs and toast in silence. On the way to the airport, he didn't say a word either. His father was quiet, too, but as they walked toward the plane, he turned to Nick and said, "This is an exciting day for you. I think you're nervous and maybe afraid. But your uncle is a competent flyer, and this is a simple, routine flight. Ask him questions. Make believe you are his copilot. That will help you feel less afraid."

"I will, Dad," Nick promised. He climbed into his uncle's plane, *The Silver Fish*. With a roar of the motor and a whir of the propellers, the plane zoomed down the airstrip. Nick, buckled in his seat, closed his eyes tightly and gripped the seat with both hands. He felt the lift of the landing gear. When the plane reached the correct altitude, his uncle said, "Open your eyes, Nick, and look out the window."

Nick glanced at his uncle's smiling face before looking out the window. But all he could see were clouds. They surrounded the plane and reminded him of that soft, squishy cotton his mother used to stuff quilts. It was fun watching them move around into different shapes. Sometimes they disappeared altogether. Soon Nick saw shimmering blue water below. How different the world seemed from above, looking down.

"You know, Nick," his uncle began, "I had to conquer my fear of flying, too. A few years back I received a distress call from Bristol Bay, a fishing village on the west coast. A man had been seriously injured there, and the fishery needed me to transport him to the Anchorage hospital. I had never landed at Bristol Bay before, but I'd heard that that landing field was really tricky. To top it off, there was a storm approaching.

"A few miles out of Anchorage, I hit the storm.

The plane started to bounce like a rubber ball. I can tell you, I was plenty scared. But then I remembered the man who would die if I didn't make that run. So I concentrated only on my flying and rode out the storm.

"You see, half of being afraid is thinking you are afraid. Now I remain calm in an emergency, and I'm always ready if the worst comes."

Nick listened calmly. He felt his body relax. After all, if Uncle Tony wasn't afraid, why should he be? He had been watching the instrument panel while his uncle talked. Never had he seen so many knobs, buttons, and lights. "What's this, Uncle Tony?" he asked, pointing to the altimeter.

"That determines our altitude. It measures the atmospheric pressure."

Nick didn't understand all his uncle said, but it didn't matter. There were more instruments to ask about, such as the compass and the turn-and-bank indicator.

"There's Kodiak Island ahead," Uncle Tony finally announced. "We'll be descending in a few minutes. Don't be nervous. Keep looking at the crab boats. Some of them are real beauties."

The Silver Fish landed right on target. It was time to unload the plane. While the fishermen piled the supplies into the loading cart, Nick bought coffee and sandwiches for them at the airport lunch counter. This pleased Uncle Tony.

Valuable time was saved.

When the cargo compartment was empty, his uncle laughed and said, "Come on, Nick. We've finished our mission. It's time we headed back home."

Nick climbed into the plane and fastened his seat belt. Somehow he felt as if he had grown six or seven inches. Within minutes *The Silver Fish* was in the air again. Nick watched the fishing boats become smaller and smaller until there was nothing but blue water below. "Wait till I tell my friends. Just wait," he said.

Going home, Nick watched the clouds and chatted with his uncle about the exciting things he'd done. Soon the lights of the Anchorage airport beckoned in the distance. "We'll be landing in a few minutes," Uncle Tony announced. They circled the field, waiting for the signal from the control tower telling them to land. Finally, clearance came. They landed and taxied up to the terminal building.

Nick saw his father waiting inside. When the door of the plane opened, Nick jumped down the steps and ran to his father. "Dad! Dad! I know what I want to be when I grow up. I want to be a pilot."

"Okay," his father answered, giving him a pat on the back. But Nick raced toward the car. There was so much to tell the others.

Gizzy and the Goozle

By Judith Ross Enderle

"Gizzy! Gizzy, child. Come here," called Aunt Sally.

Gizzy jumped from the tire swing. Red braids flying, she ran to the house. "Here I am, Aunt Sally."

"I made some corn bread," said Aunt Sally. "I want you to take a square to Grandpa Moe."

"But Grandpa Moe lives by the black swamp," said Gizzy. "And so does the goozle."

Aunt Sally shook her gray head and clucked her tongue. "Goozle foozle," she said. "That is silly talk, child. There is no such thing as a goozle."

"Kale says there is. He says it has green, shiny eyes, red fangs, a long snaky neck, a furry body, and a smell like a skunk." Gizzy shivered just thinking about it.

"The only thing that smells is that story," said Aunt Sally. "You take that bread and go before it gets dark."

"Maybe you should come along," said Gizzy hopefully. "Grandpa Moe would love to see you."

"Grandpa Moe will see me at church on Sunday," said Aunt Sally. "Now scoot." She gave Gizzy a kiss on the forehead and a pat on the shoulder.

The warm, sweet-scented square of fresh corn bread was wrapped in a checkered cloth. Gizzy held it close to her. She could feel the heat through her shirt.

"I hope the goozle doesn't like corn bread," said Gizzy as she started down the path. "I hope it doesn't like corn bread or Gizzy girls."

Along the path Gizzy heard birds and bugs. She saw lizards and a lazy snake. But she couldn't enjoy the sights. She kept thinking about that goozle. The more she thought, the more frightened she became.

A cloud covered the sun. Gizzy shivered. She began to run.

The path wound through the thick brush and past gnarled trees and all the way around the edge of the black swamp.

Out of the corner of one eye, Gizzy saw a flash of red. She smelled a potent, sour smell—somewhat like onions.

"The goozle!" she cried. Her legs went faster than she thought possible, all the way to Grandpa Moe's house.

"Gizzy girl, what's wrong? Has something happened to Aunt Sally?" Grandpa Moe asked from his porch as Gizzy came tearing up the path.

"It's the goo-goo-goozle," she gasped. "It's after me!" She pushed the square of slightly crushed corn bread at Grandpa Moe.

"Goozle, eh," said Grandpa Moe, shaking his head. "You've been listening to Kale. And Kale has been listening to Charlie Sedge."

"Charlie Sedge? You mean the tall-tale teller?" asked Gizzy.

"That's right," said Grandpa Moe.

"But I saw it," said Gizzy. "Those red fangs." She closed her eyes, remembering. "And I smelled it, too."

"Maybe," said Grandpa Moe. "We'll see. Let me put this corn bread inside. You thank Aunt Sally for me. I'll get my walking stick. Then you can show me the goozle."

Gizzy gulped. "Show you?" she squeaked.

"Yes. I'll have my stick. A goozle won't fool with Grandpa Moe's stick."

"I hope you're right," said Gizzy. She felt doubtful, but she didn't want to hurt Grandpa Moe's feelings.

Gizzy led the way back down the path around the edge of the black swamp. She stayed close to Grandpa Moe. When a bird called, Gizzy jumped.

When she came to the spot where she had seen the goozle, she pointed. "Over there," she said.

"Where?" asked Grandpa Moe.

"By the red honeysuckle."

Cautiously, Gizzy moved forward. At the edge of the path her feet flattened a skunk cabbage. The potent smell of sour onions rose up, making Gizzy choke.

But the smell was familiar. She had smelled it before. It smelled like . . . the goozle! And when she took a quick glance at the red honeysuckle flowers, they seemed like fangs.

Gizzy turned to Grandpa Moe. He wasn't laughing. He wasn't even smiling. He was just waiting.

She felt embarrassed. Then she pictured herself running scared, an imaginary monster hot on her heels. Gizzy began to laugh. She laughed until tears rolled down her cheeks. "I must have looked silly," she said, "running away from that old goozle."

"One thing Kale didn't tell you," said Grandpa Moe.

"What?" asked Gizzy.

"The goozle is afraid of people—especially little girls." Grandpa and Gizzy laughed and laughed. Their laughter filled the swamp, where some say the goozle lives.